FARM MORNING

Written and illustrated by
DAVID McPHAIL

VOYAGER BOOKS

HARCOURT BRACE & COMPANY

SAN DIEGO   NEW YORK   LONDON

FOR MY FRIENDS,
THE DELONGS —
POPPA JOHN, MOMMA PEG,
VINCENT, EVAN, AND JOHNNIE

Library of Congress Cataloging-in-Publication Data
McPhail, David M.
Farm morning.
"Voyager Books."
Summary: A father and his young daughter share a special
morning as they feed all the animals on their farm.
1. children's stories, American. [1. Fathers and
daughters—Fiction 2. Farmlife—Fiction. 3. Domestic
animals—Fiction.]. I. Title.
PZ7.M2427Far 1985   [E]   84-19167
ISBN 0-15-227299-2
ISBN 0-15-227300-X pb

I H G F E

Printed in Hong Kong

The paintings in this book were done in watercolor with
linework drawn in brown ink on 300 lb. D'Arches cold-press paper.
The text type was set on the Linotron 202 in Bembo.
The display type was filmset in Windsor Light.
Composition by Thompson Type, San Diego, California
Color separations by Heinz Weber, Inc., Los Angeles, California
Printed by South China Printing Co., Ltd., Hong Kong
Production supervision by Warren Wallerstein
Typography and binding design by Joy Chu

FARM MORNING

Even before I hear the cock crow, I hear the pit-pat,
pit-pat of little feet. "Wake up, Dad," she says.
"It's almost morning!"

The floor is cold. Summer is over . . . winter lurks.
And she has my slippers on.

Able, the cat and her accomplice,
nibbles at my ankle.
"My food, or your foot!" his
purr seems to be saying.

One of her workboots is missing. Before we can go out,
it must be found. "Here it is, under the woodstove.
Able, did you put it there?"

"All dressed? Good. Let's get started with the morning feeding!"

The squeak of the back door is the signal for the barnyard chorus to begin. (Someday I'll oil those hinges . . . and then I'll catch all those animals napping.)

The horses whinny . . .

the cow moos . . .

the sheep bleat . . .

the geese honk . . .

and the chickens carry on like old hens.
"Me, first! Me, first!" all the animals cry.

But the order of feeding is always the same: the rabbit *first*.
(Silence deserves some reward.)

Then the horses, the cow, the sheep, the geese, and the chickens—last.

"Do horses like frogs?"

"Not in their water buckets,
they don't. Horses aren't keen
on surprises."

"Do the milking? By yourself?
All right . . . but try to get
some in the pail."

"The sheep do seem to like you a lot. Maybe they think you're one of them. That's their wool you're wearing."

"Yes, I know the geese are loud. But
they might stop honking if you do."

"It's not because they're heavy that I want to carry the eggs.
 It's because they're fragile."

"See?!? Did Able put you up to this?"

"Ooops! I almost forgot the pig. (He's new.) No,
I haven't thought of a name for him yet. *Porkchop*?
I like it . . . but I don't think *he* does.

"There . . . feeding's done. But wait, haven't we
forgotten someone?"

"*Two* someones—you and me!
What would I do without you?"